A LOOK AT CONTINENTS

EXPLORE AUSTRALIA

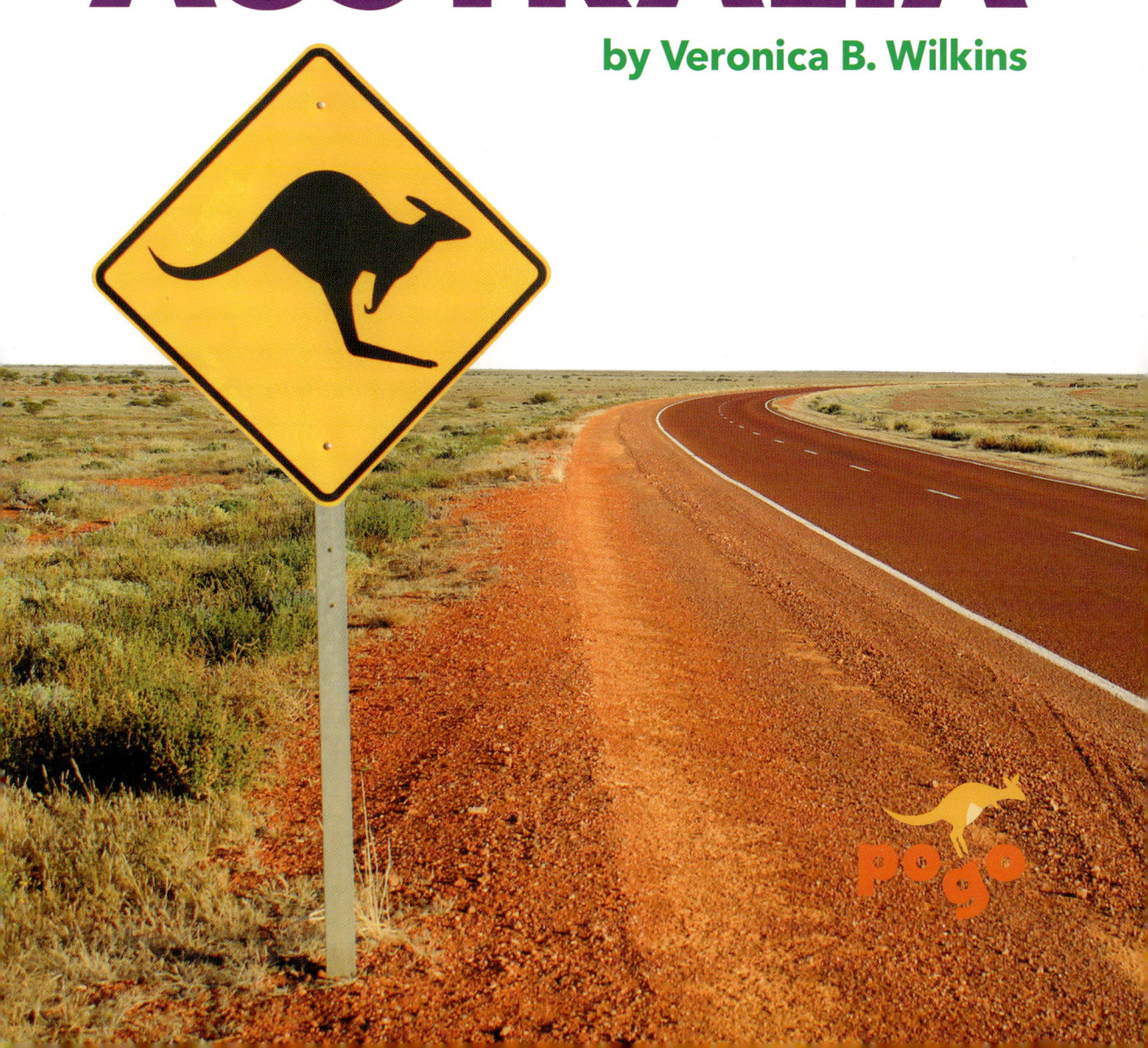

by Veronica B. Wilkins

pogo

Ideas for Parents and Teachers

Pogo Books let children practice reading informational text while introducing them to nonfiction features such as headings, labels, sidebars, maps, and diagrams, as well as a table of contents, glossary, and index.

Carefully leveled text with a strong photo match offers early fluent readers the support they need to succeed.

Before Reading

- "Walk" through the book and point out the various nonfiction features. Ask the student what purpose each feature serves.
- Look at the glossary together. Read and discuss the words.

Read the Book

- Have the child read the book independently.
- Invite him or her to list questions that arise from reading.

After Reading

- Discuss the child's questions. Talk about how he or she might find answers to those questions.
- Prompt the child to think more. Ask: There are many unique animals in Australia. What kinds of animals live near you?

Pogo Books are published by Jump!
5357 Penn Avenue South
Minneapolis, MN 55419
www.jumplibrary.com

Copyright © 2020 Jump!
International copyright reserved in all countries. No part of this book may be reproduced in any form without written permission from the publisher.

Library of Congress Cataloging-in-Publication Data is available at www.loc.gov or upon request from the publisher.

ISBN: 978-1-64527-291-5 (hardcover)
ISBN: 978-1-64527-292-2 (paperback)
ISBN: 978-1-64527-293-9 (ebook)

Editor: Susanne Bushman
Designer: Michelle Sonnek

Photo Credits: Claudio Soldi/Shutterstock, cover; Petr Kratochvila/Shutterstock, 1; Paulo Oliveira/Alamy, 3; kgrahamjourneys/iStock, 4; Debra James/Shutterstock, 5; Maciej Es/Shutterstock, 6-7 (foreground); Jaroslav74/Shutterstock, 6-7 (background); Greg Brave/Shutterstock, 8-9; Philip Schubert/Shutterstock, 10-11; Eric Isselee/Shutterstock, 12l; janaph/Shutterstock, 12r; fStop Images/Shutterstock, 13; Kima/Shutterstock, 14-15; Jeremy Red/Shutterstock, 16-17; narvikk/iStock, 18; Lisa Maree Williams/Getty, 19; Rafael Ben Ari/Dreamstime, 20-21; SeDmi/Shutterstock, 23.

Printed in the United States of America at Corporate Graphics in North Mankato, Minnesota.

TABLE OF CONTENTS

CHAPTER 1
Australian Landscape 4

CHAPTER 2
Animals of the Outback 12

CHAPTER 3
Life in Australia 18

QUICK FACTS & TOOLS
At a Glance 22
Glossary 23
Index 24
To Learn More 24

CHAPTER 1
AUSTRALIAN LANDSCAPE

Let's explore the **continent** of Australia! This is Lake Saint Clair. It is Australia's deepest lake. It some areas, it is 700 feet (213 meters) deep!

Lake Saint Clair

The Great Barrier Reef is here. It is the largest **coral reef** in the world. It is more than 1,250 miles (2,012 kilometers) long! Around 1,500 types of fish live here!

CHAPTER 1 5

Australia is the smallest continent. It is south of the **equator**. It is in the Southern **Hemisphere**.

Australia is the name of a country and a continent. There are many islands in the Pacific Ocean near Australia. This area is called Oceania. More than 10,000 islands make up this **region**. The islands of New Zealand are some of the largest.

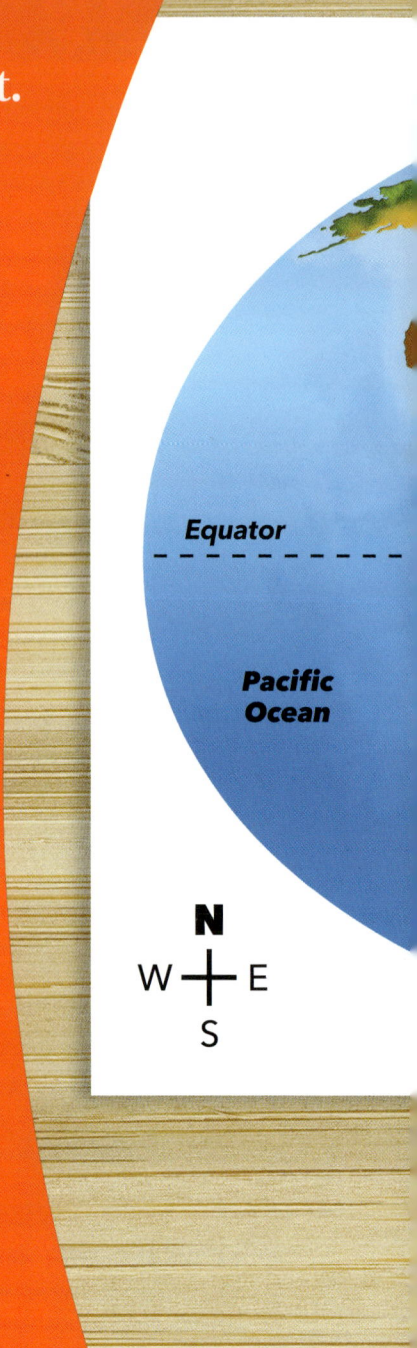

CHAPTER 1

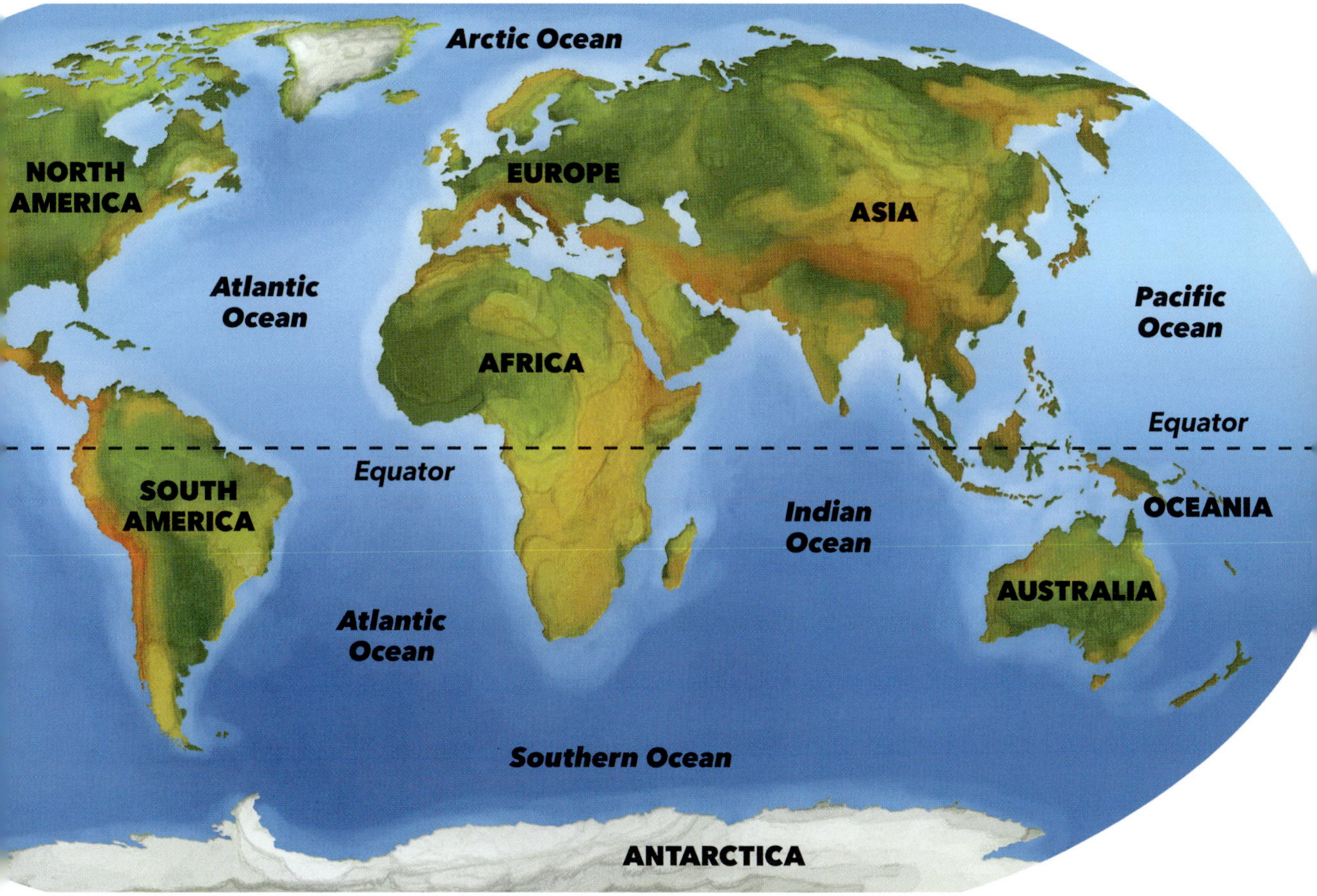
Arctic Ocean
NORTH AMERICA
EUROPE
ASIA
Atlantic Ocean
Pacific Ocean
AFRICA
Equator
SOUTH AMERICA
Equator
Indian Ocean
OCEANIA
AUSTRALIA
Atlantic Ocean
Southern Ocean
ANTARCTICA

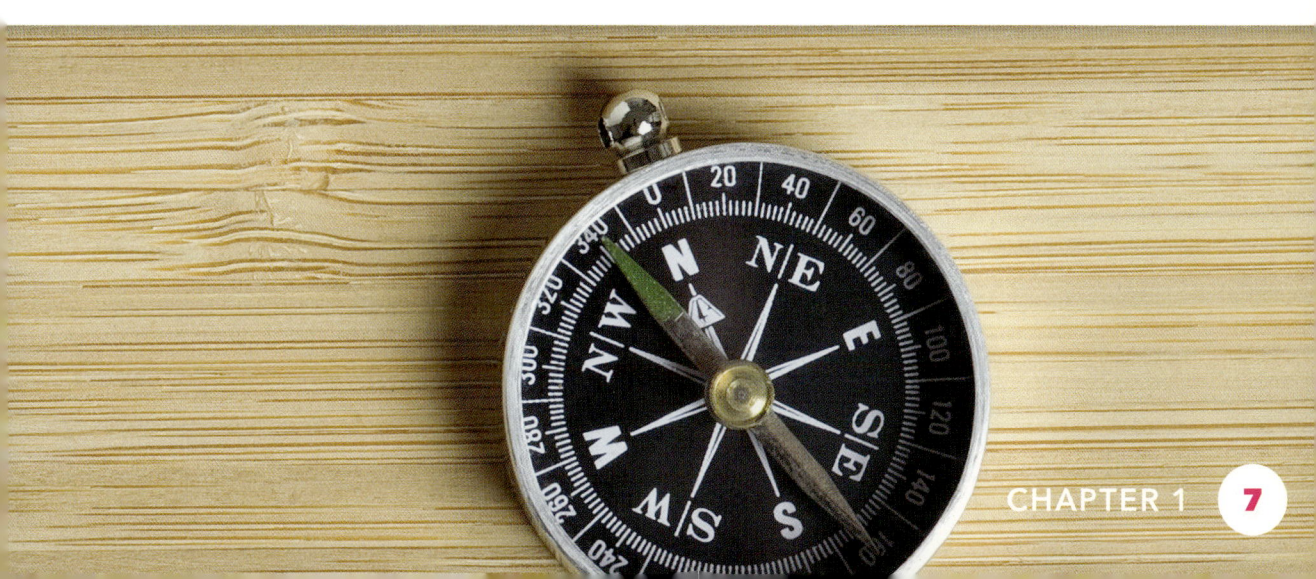

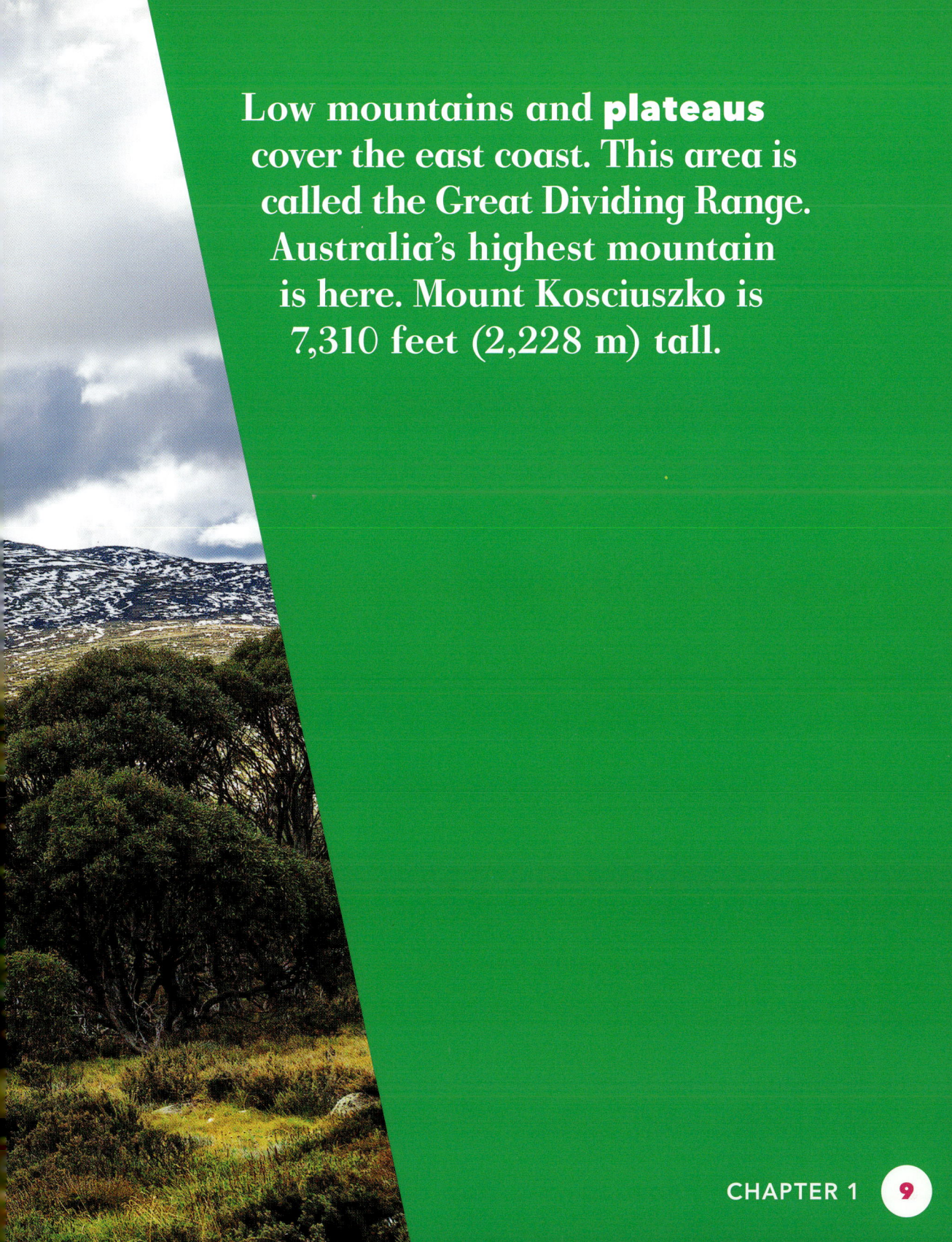

Low mountains and **plateaus** cover the east coast. This area is called the Great Dividing Range. Australia's highest mountain is here. Mount Kosciuszko is 7,310 feet (2,228 m) tall.

This is the flattest continent. It is covered in large **plains** and **deserts**. People call these **rural** areas the Outback.

The Great Victoria Desert is in the south. The Kimberleys are in the northwest. Deep **gorges** are here.

WHAT DO YOU THINK?

Coober Pedy is a town in the desert. Many buildings are underground. Why? It is too hot above ground! Would you like to live here?

CHAPTER 2
ANIMALS OF THE OUTBACK

Many animals here are unique to this continent. Koalas munch on eucalyptus.

Kangaroos roam. They hop on their back legs. Mothers carry their babies in pouches. They are called joeys.

joey

CHAPTER 2

Platypuses swim in lakes and rivers. Echidna crawl slowly on land. They are covered in pointy spines. These spines keep them safe from other animals. They catch food with their long beaks.

DID YOU KNOW?

Echidna and platypuses are special. Why? They are the only **mammals** that lay eggs!

14 CHAPTER 2

echidna

CHAPTER 2 · 15

The **climate** here is dry. Most places get little rain. Summers are very hot. It is often hotter than 100 degrees Fahrenheit (38 degrees Celsius). The coasts are cooler. Why? The ocean creates cool air.

TAKE A LOOK!

What are the climate regions of Australia? Take a look!

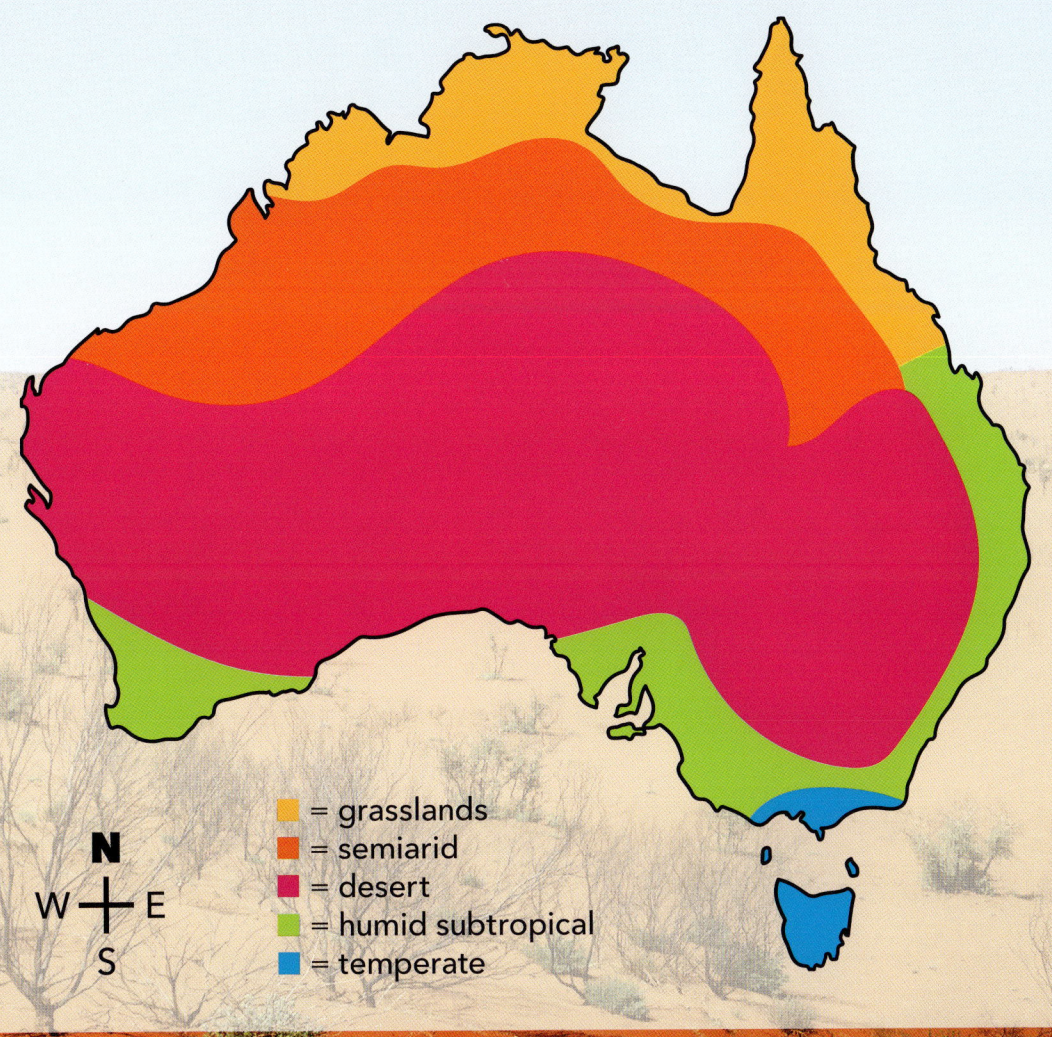

= grasslands
= semiarid
= desert
= humid subtropical
= temperate

CHAPTER 2

CHAPTER 3
LIFE IN AUSTRALIA

Most people here live in cities. Sydney has the most people. More than five million people live here!

Sydney

Few people live in the Outback. Many who do have large ranches. Ranchers raise sheep and cattle. Others grow **crops**, like sugarcane and wheat.

CHAPTER 3

More than 270 **ethnic** groups live here. Many people speak English. But there are many **Aboriginal** languages, too. Aboriginal peoples celebrate their **cultures**. Some dance in traditional outfits.

Australia has many amazing sights. Would you like to explore this continent?

CHAPTER 3 — 21

QUICK FACTS & TOOLS

AT A GLANCE

AUSTRALIA

Size: 2,969,976 square miles (7,692,202 square kilometers)

Size Rank: Asia, Africa, North America, South America, Antarctica, Europe, **Australia**

Population Estimate: 25 million people (2019 estimate)

Exports: iron ore, coal, gold, natural gas, beef

Facts: Australia makes up five percent of Earth's land.

Australia has the world's largest sand island. Fraser Island is 75 miles (121 km) long.

GLOSSARY

Aboriginal: The native people of Australia who have lived there since before the Europeans arrived.

climate: The weather typical of a certain place over a long period of time.

continent: One of the seven large landmasses of Earth.

coral reef: A strip of coral close to the surface of the ocean or another body of water.

crops: Plants grown for food.

cultures: The ideas, customs, traditions, and ways of life of groups of people.

deserts: Dry areas where hardly any plants grow because there is so little rain.

equator: An imaginary line around the middle of Earth that is an equal distance from the North and South Poles.

ethnic: Of or having to do with a group of people sharing the same national origins, language, or culture.

gorges: Deep valleys with steep, rocky sides.

hemisphere: Half of a round object, especially of Earth.

mammals: Warm-blooded animals with hair or fur that usually give birth to live babies.

plains: Large, flat areas of land.

plateaus: Areas of level ground that are higher than the surrounding areas.

region: A general area or a specific district or territory.

rural: Related to the country and country life.

QUICK FACTS & TOOLS

INDEX

animals 5, 12, 13, 14, 19
climate 16, 17
climate regions 17
Coober Pedy 10
deserts 10
equator 6
ethnic groups 21
Great Barrier Reef 5
Great Dividing Range 9
Great Victoria Desert 10
islands 6
Kimberleys 10
Lake Saint Clair 4
languages 21
mammals 14
Mount Kosciuszko 9
New Zealand 6
Oceania 6
Outback 10, 19
Pacific Ocean 6
people 10, 18, 19, 21
plains 10
plateaus 9
Southern Hemisphere 6

TO LEARN MORE

Finding more information is as easy as 1, 2, 3.

❶ Go to www.factsurfer.com
❷ Enter "exploreAustralia" into the search box.
❸ Choose your book to see a list of websites.